Cuckold's Anonymous

Wanda Peters

Published by Wanda Peters, 2020.

CUCKOLD'S ANONYMOUS

First edition. June 21, 2020.

ISBN: 979-8227535030

Written by Wanda Peters.

Also by Wanda Peters

10 Reasons You Should Cuckold Your Husband
Cruel Wife, Slave Husband
Embracing My Inner Bitch
Erotic Short Stories of Dominance and Submission
My Evil Step-Sister Returns Illustrated
Cuckolded By A Stranger, An Erotic Novel
Cuckolded By His Boss
The Hot Wife Club
Cuckolded and Bound for Punishment
Cuckolded By My Best Friend
Cuckold's Anonymous
An Anniversary To Remember
My Wife's Surprise
Terrified of Bondage A Wife in Peril
Training Her Cuckold Husband
A Little Devil in Georgia
His Mother's Advice
Addicted To High Heels or A Slave To My Wife's Boots
The Huntress
A Wedding to Remember
Evil Under a Western Sky
The Number Four Reason You Should Cuckold Your Husband
Cuckolding The Bootlicker
Bondage and Discipline 101
Tales of Love Romance and Marriage

Tales of Love, Romance and Marriage
The Evil Therapist Returns
Cracks in the Vow Six Stories of Love's Demise
Two Books Of Domination And Legal Thrillers
An Old Flame For Ava
An Interview With An Erotic Writer
Bound For Desire
The Awakening- Susan's Path to Sensual Empowerment

Cuckold's Anonymous
Wanda Peters
Copyright 2014
Smashwords Edition

Disclaimer. The book is a work of fiction. Any resemblance to anyone living or dead is merely a coincidence. It is intended for mature audiences only as it contains adult language, depictions of sexual activity, and some violence. If these things offend you, please do not read this book. All images in this book have been AI generated and have no copywrites attached.

Cuckold's Anonymous

Chapter One – Exploring Forbidden Desires, Inside Cuckold's Anonymous

The room was like any other used by 12-step programs. Rows of hard folding chairs were arranged neatly, all facing the podium at the front. In one corner, a small table held a large coffee pot, a welcome addition for those in attendance. As I entered, I couldn't help but notice that only about half of the chairs were occupied. People sat scattered throughout the room, keeping their distance from one another. It was clear they were here for a common purpose, but not to form close bonds.

I walked to an empty chair and took a seat, observing as newcomers trickled in. This was my first time attending this particular group, though I had been to several Alcoholics Anonymous meetings before. I assumed it would be similar - someone would announce when it was time to start, possibly with a prayer or benediction like the "Serenity Prayer." Then one by one, people would share their confessions and struggles with addiction or weakness.

Upon closer inspection, I noticed a woman sitting by herself in the back row, as far away from the podium as possible. Her presence intrigued me - what was her story? Did she come here alone? My curiosity tempted me to approach her, but before I could make a move, the microphone came alive and silenced any potential disruptions. With a quick scan of the room, I realized that everyone else seemed settled into their seats and ready to begin. I reminded myself that I was only here to observe and take notes - sharing wasn't part of my agenda tonight. But as the meeting proceeded and individuals bravely shared their struggles and sorrows, I couldn't help but feel drawn in by their honesty and vulnerability. By the end of the night, despite my initial intentions, I found myself feeling grateful for being a part of this group's journey towards recovery and healing.

A tall, lean man stood behind a microphone, tapping the end to capture everyone's attention. The room fell quiet as all eyes turned towards him, waiting for his next words. "I want to extend a warm welcome to each and every one of you tonight. Our meeting will begin shortly, but before we do, I must ask someone to leave. Marcie, I see you in the back corner. You know this is a closed meeting for members of the female sex. Would you please make this easy on everyone and vacate the meeting room?"

The atmosphere in the room shifted as all heads turned to look at the woman in question. After a pregnant pause, she rose from her seat but made no move towards the exit. I couldn't help but study her appearance and demeanor. She seemed slightly overdressed for the occasion, but not enough to seem out of place. Her plain cotton dress came down below her knees and buttoned high on her neck, leaving no exposed skin. Her hair was neatly styled into a bun at the nape of her neck, and she wore a string of large pearls around it. Her feet were hidden from view, but I assumed she was wearing flats based on her sturdy stance with her feet together. Had she been wearing heels, she would have had to shift her weight outward to maintain balance. Her makeup was minimal, though her lips did have a hint of pink that suggested she may be wearing lipstick. In all, she was quite attractive but not overtly trying to draw attention.

Finally, she spoke up in defiance. "Bill, we've been over this before. I have just as much right to be here as any other member of this group. How do you know I don't have something valuable to contribute?"

"Because you're a woman," he sneered back at her. "That's why. How can these men open up and share their experiences if one of the people responsible for their suffering is in the room?"

A flicker of pain flashed across her face before she composed herself. "I don't recall you having any trouble talking to me when we were married. I'm not leaving until I'm good and ready. You could call the police, but we both know they won't come. We've been through that charade before. Now, why don't you start the meeting? Maybe I'll contribute, maybe I won't."

Admiration stirred within me as I watched her, a firecracker of a woman with unbreakable determination. When the meeting eventually ended, I knew I had to spend some time talking with her.

Bill's defeated expression gave away that he was used to being under her thumb. His wife's remark about their past marriage hinted that this was not the first time she had tamed him, perhaps even physically. "Let's all calm down now," Bill spoke up. "We'll just have to ignore Marci and carry on as if she's not here. Let us begin with the serenity prayer."

I bowed my head, not out of reverence but simply to blend in with the rest of the congregation. The words of the prayer were familiar to me, having heard them countless times before. I was relieved when it ended quickly, eager to move on to the reason we were all gathered here.

Once everyone had said their amens, Bill addressed the group again. "I see there are some new faces tonight. Would anyone like to introduce themselves?" He deliberately avoided making eye contact with anyone, but his gaze seemed to land directly on me. To avoid drawing attention to myself, I decided to go along with his request rather than trying to evade it.

Standing up, I cleared my throat and spoke into the silence. "Hello, my name is Jack." A chorus of voices echoed back at me: "Hi, Jack." I couldn't help but be grateful that we weren't in a crowded airport or bus terminal. "This is my first time here and I'm just observing for now.

Perhaps I may share something another time." With that, I sat back down without looking left or right.

"Alright then," Bill continued, addressing the group once more. "Does anyone have anything they would like to share tonight?"

Chapter Two Roger's Revelations: A Cuckold's Journey

The room fell silent as the short, pudgy man made his way towards the podium and microphone. His every step seemed to carry a weight of sadness and defeat. "Most of you know me," he began in a resigned tone. "My name is Roger, and I am a cuckold."

"Hi, Roger," echoed throughout the room, a symphony of pity and camaraderie.

As Roger launched into his tale of woe, I couldn't help but feel a pang of sympathy for him. It was clear that he was no longer living with the woman who had turned him into a cuckold, but it seemed that once someone entered this realm, they were forever marked by it. With trembling hands and tears in his eyes, Roger shared the struggles he faced after deciding to leave his cheating wife. He had very little possessions or finances and had resorted to seeking shelter at a battered men's facility, though he did not disclose what kind of abuse he suffered at the hands of his unfaithful spouse.

Personally, I found Roger's story rather dull. I yearned for more details about how he came to be a cuckold, rather than just hearing about the aftermath. But I knew that due to the confidentiality rules of this group, I would only hear the full story from one person - unless Roger himself was willing to share.

Thankfully, Roger eventually finished speaking and another man took his place at the podium. This man caught my attention immediately

- towering at six-foot-four and weighing at least 220 pounds of pure muscle. His short-sleeved shirt strained against his biceps and his neck looked like it could rival that of a bull's. And yet, despite his impressive physical appearance, there was a hint of vulnerability in his voice as he introduced himself.

"Hi, my name is Phil, and I am a cuckold," he stated confidently, though a tinge of shame seeped through his words. In unison, the group responded with the obligatory "Hi Phil."

"This is my first time here," Phil continued, "so I guess I should share a bit about myself before getting to where I am now." He took a deep breath before launching into his story. Ten years ago, he married what he believed to be the sweetest and most loving woman in the world. He had loved her so deeply that he would do anything for her - even now, despite everything that happened, he still longed for her to take him back.

The early years of our marriage were filled with joy and hope. We dreamed of starting a family, but despite our efforts, we couldn't seem to conceive. Frustrated and desperate for answers, we turned to a fertility doctor. The results were devastating - I was diagnosed as sterile, with an abnormally low sperm count. It was a blow to my ego and our dreams.

We discussed alternative options like adoption or artificial insemination, but Charlotte refused to consider them. She wanted a child who shared her DNA, and she blamed me for the infertility issue. Many arguments ensued, each one more heated than the last. I tried to reason with her, but she wouldn't budge from her position.

Eventually, we reached a fragile truce, but it didn't repair the distance that had grown between us. Our physical intimacy dwindled, and when we did have sex, it felt rushed and lacking in passion. Meanwhile, Charlotte started spending more time with her friends. At first, it was just casual outings once a month, then twice a month, and eventually every week without telling me where she was going or what they were doing.

I'll admit, I didn't think much of it until I noticed how she started dressing differently for these outings. Her clothes became more revealing - short skirts that showed off garters instead of pantyhose and sheer blouses that left little to the imagination. And her shoes...they went from practical flats to dangerously high heels that screamed "seduction." It was like she had gone back in time to our honeymoon phase.

One night, as she was getting ready for yet another evening out with her friends, I couldn't help but comment on how provocative she looked. But instead of engaging in a conversation, she simply blew me a kiss and left without saying anything else. "Don't wait up," she called out as she closed the door behind her. Little did I know, that would be the last time things felt somewhat normal between us.

The soft glow of the television flickered in the dark room as I sat, nursing a few drinks. Curiosity nagged at me, and I couldn't resist going up to our bedroom and rummaging through her drawers. They were filled with lacy lingerie, all from Victoria's Secret, and my mind began to race with suspicion. Who was she buying these for? It certainly wasn't for me.

My suspicions grew when she didn't come home that night or the next. When I finally saw her on Sunday afternoon, she looked like she had been through hell and back. Her hair was disheveled, her clothes wrinkled, and there were bruises on her skin.

I confronted her, demanding to know where she had been and who she had been with. But all she said was that I didn't want to know, and she wanted to be left alone to sleep in peace. That's when I made the move into the guest room permanent.

I still didn't have proof of her infidelity, but all signs pointed towards it. So I hired a private investigator to follow her the next weekend. And what they found broke my heart.

She met with my best friend at a motel, where they spent the entire weekend together. The investigator managed to snap photos of them kissing like lovesick teenagers.

At this point in his story, tears began to fall from Bill's eyes and he asked someone else to share. Another man named Fred took the floor and started speaking, causing me to tune out initially. But then he said something that caught my attention.

"I am here because of my foolishness," Fred confessed. "I had this idea that it would be thrilling to watch my wife with another man. Maybe it came from browsing the wrong sites on the Internet or maybe I sought out those sites because the idea was already in my head. Either way, in every fantasy I read online, the couple always ended up happy in the end. The woman gets to enjoy a lover on the side, and the husband is grateful just to watch or participate."

I hesitantly brought up the topic with my wife, bracing myself for her reaction. She immediately accused me of losing my mind and urged me to seek psychiatric help. But I persisted, asking if she had ever fantasized about being with another man, someone younger and more physically fit, someone with a strong, impressive physique.

Surprisingly, she seemed intrigued by this idea and joked that I should go find someone like that for her. However, she warned that she wouldn't settle for anything less than perfection. We laughed at the absurdity of it all before she walked away, probably to look up the number for a mental institution.

Despite knowing better, I couldn't let the idea go and continued to search the internet for ideas. The thought of seeing my wife in the arms of another man, experiencing pleasure I could not provide, consumed me. It was ridiculous and foolish, but I couldn't stop myself.

Suddenly, a loud sound of hands clapping echoed from the back corner of the room, followed by a woman's voice cheering in agreement. Fred paused his story and acknowledged Marcie, inviting her to speak her mind. But before she could say anything else, Bill shut her down and reminded everyone to focus on Fred's story.

But Marcie couldn't be silenced. She spoke out against the men in the room who pushed their wives into infidelity and then were surprised by their actions. She challenged Bill's authority and encouraged Fred to continue his story. I smirked inwardly as I realized she may have orchestrated this entire situation.

Fred started his story again, admitting that he was blinded by his own desires and did not think about the consequences of bringing another person into their marriage. He learned the hard way that introducing a third party into a relationship can do more harm than good.

As he finished speaking and made his way back to his seat, Marcie stood up once again and applauded him. I couldn't help but wonder if there was more to their story than what Fred was sharing with us.

Chapter Three- Tangled Desires Unveiled: Secrets of a Cuckoldress

The meeting dragged on for what seemed like hours, with each speaker going on and on about their struggles and challenges. I stayed behind after the adjournment, hoping to catch someone's attention and maybe strike up a conversation. But the group was tight-knit, only conversing when they had a microphone in their hands.

I glanced around the room, searching for Marcie. She was nowhere to be found, probably avoiding any possible confrontation with her ex-husband. With no one to talk to, I headed towards the exit. No one stopped me or said goodbye, unlike the warm atmosphere of an Alcoholics Anonymous meeting where every member was like family.

As I stepped out into the dimly lit parking lot, I noticed a figure leaning against my car in the far corner. A cigarette glowed in the darkness, giving away their presence. In this group, it was uncommon to see someone smoking, unlike at AA meetings where everyone chain-smoked while drinking endless amounts of coffee.

Nervousness crept over me as I approached my car. I couldn't recall doing anything that would warrant someone waiting for me in the dark. But in this world, you can never be too careful.

My apprehension eased as I saw who was leaning against my car: Marcie. Her relaxed posture reassured me that she didn't have any issues with me.

"I thought you had left," I greeted her as I reached my car. She took my hand in a firm handshake, surprising me with her strength.

"Yes, I heard your introduction at the meeting. Do you have trouble getting through airport security?"

I chuckled at the old joke, having heard it countless times before. "And you must be Marcie? Are you waiting for me or just using my car as a leaning post?"

She smirked and shook her head. "No, I wanted to welcome you to the group. Though I have a feeling you don't really belong here."

"Why do you say that? What other reason would I have for attending this meeting?"

"Well, for one thing, you seemed too interested in what everyone was saying. And yes, before you ask, I have been keeping an eye on you."

I couldn't help but ask, "Can you please explain why?"

She looked at me with a hint of amusement in her eyes. "For starters, you don't quite fit the image of a typical cuckold. And I'm sure you're dying to know this, so I'll answer before you even ask. Most cuckolds have a sad and defeated look, especially when they're around women. But when Bill and I were arguing, you didn't flinch. You stared me down like I was just another person in the crowd, not your mortal enemy."

"So what's your theory about why I'm here? Do you think I might be a married man wanting to explore having my wife cuckold me, I want to know all the details before I make a decision?"

She laughed. "Highly unlikely. I think you have an entirely different agenda. Are you a journalist or a novelist trying to gather material for a story?"

"If that were true, do you think I'd be successful in my venture?"

"It depends on whether or not you buy me a drink. I've heard plenty of stories, but we can't stand here in this parking lot and talk about them all."

"Do you have a preference for where we get that drink?"

"If you're single, let's go to your place. If not, then we'll go to mine."

"My place it is. I hope bourbon or beer is okay because those are my only options unless you want coffee or water."

"Bourbon is perfect. My car is over there." She pointed off to my left. "Just give me a moment to start it up, and then I'll follow you."

As she walked away, I couldn't help but admire the way her hips swayed with each step. Even though she wasn't dressed provocatively, she had a natural sensuality that couldn't be ignored. It made me think how foolish Bill was to want to share her with another man. Once she was safely in her car, I got into mine and backed out of my parking spot. I drove towards the exit, keeping an eye on my rearview mirror to make sure she was following. I didn't want to lose this woman before we had a chance to get to know each other better. And by "get to know each other better," I meant much more intimate than just exchanging pleasantries.

It only took about 15 minutes to reach my apartment. It wasn't enough time for me to come up with a well-thought-out plan for what I was going to say or how I would say it, but it was long enough for me to outline some rough ideas. Since she already suspected me of being a reporter, I figured I might as well do something I rarely did – tell her the truth and see where it led us.

Parking my car in a designated guest space in the apartment lot, I eagerly awaited Marcie's arrival. Once she pulled up beside me and turned off her engine, I quickly exited my car and went to help her out. She graciously accepted my hand and emerged from the vehicle, giving it a gentle push before locking it with her key fob. Offering her my arm, I led her across the asphalt towards the narrow walkway between buildings in the large complex.

As we walked, neither of us spoke, taking in the sights and sounds of the bustling community. Finally reaching my front stoop, I reached for my keys and unlocked the door, flipping on the light inside. Stepping back, I gestured for Marcie to enter first.

She stepped into my modestly furnished kitchen and allowed me to follow before stopping to take in the decor. Hoping that she wouldn't be disappointed, I offered to give her a tour of my small apartment.

"Would you like to see around or head straight to the living room? It'll only take a minute or two."

"Why don't we save time and just go to the living room? I'm here for the alcohol after all," she replied with a playful smile.

Leading her into the cozy living room, I offered her a choice between an armchair and the sofa. She chose the latter and situated herself comfortably in the center of the piece. Fixing us both drinks, I returned to find her settled in with her legs tucked under her and shoes neatly placed in front of her.

Taking a seat at a comfortable distance from her on the sofa, I couldn't help but wonder if she was purposely monopolizing the furniture or inviting me to sit closer. Regardless, I handed her a drink and settled in beside her.

"So why are we here again?" I asked curiously.

"Well, it seems you want some information from me, and in exchange, I want to know why. How about you tell me what you're looking for and then I'll share what I know?" she proposed.

"Fair enough," I agreed. "You were close in your assumption - I am a reporter, but not for a magazine or paper. I'm a freelance writer, making a modest living by writing articles on topics of public interest. Recently, I did a piece on a man who committed suicide after discovering his wife's affair. But upon further investigation, it seemed he may have been the one who suggested the affair in the first place. This led me to look into cuckolding and eventually brought me to your group. Of course, I've researched countless websites dedicated to hot wives and submissive men, but many seem fake."

"Why would you say that?" she asked me.

"Many of the stories revolved around men who took pleasure in watching their wives engage in sexual acts with other men. The women, hesitant at first, would eventually give in and become unable to resist participating further. But despite these actions, they professed to still love their husbands. While some of the stories depicted cruel intentions, others showed a loving dynamic between the couples. And yet, all of them claimed that their marriages were somehow improved by taking on a lover.

"Do any of these stories ring true to you?" I asked.

"I'm sure there are bits and pieces of truth mixed in with a lot of lies," she replied coolly. "Those Internet sites exist for the sole purpose of titillating men, and perhaps a few women as well. But the majority of those sites are created by men, for the gratification of other men. Of course, many claim to be written by women, but if you read closely, it's easy to tell when the writer has little knowledge of female anatomy."

"I see," I said, getting her point.

"For instance," she continued, "when you were reading those blogs, did any of them mention how the wife would come home with her vagina filled with her lover's ejaculate and then force her husband to clean it up?" She raised an eyebrow expectantly.

I nodded slowly. "Yes, that seemed to be a recurring theme."

"Well," she said knowingly, "a woman would know that ejaculate begins breaking down after just a few minutes. By the time she got home to her husband, most - if not all - of it would have leaked out. He may get a taste, but certainly not a full meal. These are just small details that give away the phoniness of these stories. Now," she leaned forward slightly, "would you like to hear some true stories?"

I reached for my recorder and turned it on excitedly. "I don't want to miss a single word of your narrative."

She nodded and began. "Let me start with a story that I know to be true. Do you remember the one Fred started telling towards the end of our meeting?"

I thought back for a moment before nodding. "Yes, I do. You seemed quite pleased with his confession."

"Indeed," she smiled wryly. "Mainly because what he said was completely honest. I can't say if he would have continued being truthful, but everything he did say was true - at least up until that point. And I know this because it was exactly how my husband and I started our journey. When we first got married, we had sex constantly. Before I knew it, we were averaging six times a week, maybe even more. Of course, men tend to keep track of those things more than women, so his number might differ from mine." She chuckled softly before continuing.

"But what truly mattered to me was not the frequency or duration of our sexual encounters, but rather the time and effort my husband put into pleasuring me. He was always attentive and never rushed me, taking his time to bring me to the brink and back down again. And despite what he may have believed about himself, his size was never an issue for me. It was all the other activities leading up to intercourse that truly mattered."

She paused, collecting her thoughts before continuing. Her fingers fidgeted with the hem of her skirt as she mentally prepared for what she was about to reveal. I gave her a moment, sensing that there was more to the story than what she had already shared.

"Well," she began again, "as our marriage grew older, things changed. The absence of children wasn't the only obstacle we faced. Two jobs, a barely affordable mortgage, and two cars to maintain took up most of our energy and time. Sex became less frequent and passion dwindled. What used to be multiple earth-shattering orgasms turned into one mild ripple. And suddenly, I found myself losing interest. It wasn't all Bill's fault - we both played a role in the decline. But he seemed to take it harder than I did."

I noticed her glass and mine were empty, so I offered to get another round.

"Another drink would be lovely, and an ashtray if you don't mind me smoking."

I granted her permission and headed to the kitchen. Returning with two stiff drinks and a small dish serving as an ashtray, I watched as she carefully lit a cigarette and drew the smoke into her lungs. She held it there for a moment before exhaling through her nose. Handing her the drink, I set the ashtray down on the coffee table in front of her.

"I take it you don't smoke," she observed.

"I used to, but when cigarettes hit $4 a pack, I had to choose between nicotine or food. I chose food."

"I know what you mean. Luckily, I found an Indian smoke shop on the reservation just outside of the city. I can get two cartons for just over $60 total. Still not cheap, but it's my only expensive habit. And funny enough, smoking was something I picked up from my lover - at Bill's insistence."

"Ah, so you still see the other man," I interjected.

"That's getting ahead of the story. Let me stick to chronological order if you don't mind."

"Of course, please continue."

She chuckled and said, "Sorry, I already got ahead of myself when I mentioned taking a lover."

"I gathered as much from listening to you and Bill at the meeting. Don't worry about it. Do you need a break?"

She glanced at her watch and replied, "No, I'm fine for now. But it is getting late and I don't want to keep you past your bedtime.

I could see the invitation in her eyes and I got up and moved to where she was sitting on the sofa. I sat down beside her and drew her to me.

Leaning in, I brushed a strand of hair away from her face and whispered, "I don't mind staying up a bit longer."

A smile played on her lips as she gazed into my eyes, her own sparkling with a mix of emotions. The room was filled with the soft glow of the lamp casting shadows around us, creating an intimate atmosphere that seemed to draw us closer together.

As our lips met in a gentle kiss, I felt a surge of warmth flood through me, igniting a passion that had been simmering beneath the surface. Her hands found their way to my shoulders, pulling me closer as the kiss deepened, becoming more urgent and fervent.

Time seemed to stand still as we lost ourselves in each other, the outside world fading away until there was only the two of us, locked in an embrace that spoke volumes without words. And in that moment, I knew that this was just the beginning of a story that was yet to unfold.

My fingers danced along the hem of her blouse, their tips grazing the skin beneath. Our kisses were akin to a wildfire, spreading heat through our bodies as they ignited sparks in places untread for too long. The taste of whiskey and cigarettes on her lips intoxicated me more than any drink could, fueling my desire even further.

Hesitant and eager all at once, I unbuttoned her blouse with deft precision, revealing the lacy bra that cradled her supple breasts. My hands trembled with anticipation as I traced the outline of her curves, feeling her heart pound against my palm in rhythm with mine.

"You're beautiful," I murmured against her ear, tracing its delicate shell with my tongue. The words weren't enough to encapsulate what she was - a goddess clothed in ethereal beauty - but it was all I could say without losing myself completely.

Her laughter sent waves of desire coursing through me, filling me with an ache only she could extinguish. With one swift move, I unclasped her bra, releasing her twin peaks into the chill.

My gaze dropped to her pert nipples begging for attention. Taking one in my mouth, I teased it with slow swirls before lightly nibbling on it. Her gasps and moans were like erotic music to my ears; each breathy noise made me crave more of her essence.

"Please," she whispered, pressing herself onto me in a plea that didn't need translation. My fingers began their journey downward from there, tracing her flat stomach before dipping below the waistband of her skirt.

I unlatched her belt buckle expertly before wrestling her skirt down past her thighs. As I devoured the sight of black lace panties hugging snugly against her mound, my trousers became unbearably tight around my bulging arousal.

With trembling hands fiddling with the button of my pants, I finally gave in and let them drop down. The chill of the room swept me, contrasting with the heat radiating from her skin. My cock throbbed against my boxers, aching to delve into her depths.

"Let's not keep this waiting," she smirked, hooking a finger around the hem of my boxers before dragging them down mercilessly. Our bodies hummed in unison as we tumbled onto the bed, wrapped around each other in a feverish embrace.

My fingers dipped into her wetness while my mouth claimed her nipple once again. Her body undulated beneath mine conspiring with her moans that filled the room. I devoured every gasp, every whimper that escaped from her lips, storing it away like an addict.

"I want you now," I rasped against her earlobe, drawing a shudder from her. She responded by locking her legs around my waist, pulling me closer until there was no space left between us.

Our bodies found a rhythm in each other's movements as if entranced in a carnal dance; one that spoke volumes of untamed desires and pent-up frustrations. We rode on waves of pleasure until they crashed upon our shores leaving nothing but blissful satisfaction in its wake.

Every bone in our bodies seemed to melt into each other as we reveled in newfound ecstasy. As we lay tangled together amidst scattered clothes and tousled sheets, we breathed in sync. Each breath carried remnants of our desire for each other – raw and intense.

This was just the beginning of exploring each other's bodies; an uncovering of secrets better felt than said. And I knew then that no erotica could ever measure up to what reality offered us - a taste of foreplay laced with fiery passion.

Slowing down to savor the moment, I began to explore her body with my hands, tracing every curve and dip of her ribcage. My mouth found its way back to her breasts, softly kissing and nipping at them while she reached between us to find what she was looking for. A surge of pleasure ran through me as she squeezed at the base of my erection and gently pulled upward, causing it to throb even harder. Our moans mingled together in perfect harmony.

In a blur of movement, she slipped out of my grip and positioned herself on her knees with her mouth hovering over my cock. Meanwhile, my mouth was just inches away from the most beautiful pussy I had seen in years. Without hesitation, I reached up and gripped both of her ass cheeks, pulling her down until I could run my tongue along the folds of her dripping wetness. Slowly and deliberately, I explored every inch of her slick entrance before finally plunging my tongue inside, relishing in the powerful taste of her musky sweetness.

Not one to be outdone, she lavished attention on my throbbing cock with her mouth - teasing and tantalizing me with each stroke of her tongue. We were both overcome with pleasure and desire as she switched positions and impaled herself onto my aching erection. Her aim was spot on as she rode me deeper and deeper until I was fully engulfed in her warm wetness. A slight twitch ran through us both as we stayed still, savoring the intimate connection between us. Then she began to move, grinding herself against my pelvis while her tight walls squeezed and massaged me with each thrust. No longer unsure, she had become an expert in the art of fucking, taking us both on a wild and exhilarating ride of pleasure.

I studied her intently as she lay there, vulnerable and open to me. Her breasts heaving with each breath - those perfectly formed mounds of feminine beauty that had earlier been moving rhythmically up and down with her laughter were now still, except for the occasional shiver. Each nipple pointed upwards like taut sentinels standing at attention in a sea of creamy white skin. The faint scent of our shared carnal escapades still lingered between us, mingling with the musky aroma of arousal.

Sex-soaked and sated, we lay there panting – a tangled mess beneath the covers staring at each other wordlessly. Sweet exhaustion settled over us as we snuggled closer; our hearts still racing from that mind-blowing orgasm.

"I guess this is what makes you special," I whispered into her ear after a while. "You make simple sex feel like an extraordinary experience."

Chapter Four - The Next Day Marci's Story Continues

The warmth of her body pressed against mine brought a sense of contentment that I had never experienced before. As the morning light filtered through the curtains, I couldn't help but admire the peaceful expression on her face as she slept. The soft curves of her body were like a work of art, and I felt grateful to be able to share this intimate moment with her.

But eventually, nature called and I was forced to untangle myself from her embrace. She stirred slightly as I slipped out of bed, but thankfully did not fully awaken. In the bathroom, I took a moment to appreciate my own nakedness and how comfortable I now felt being vulnerable in front of someone I had only met yesterday.

When I returned to the bedroom, Marci was already sitting up in bed, modestly covering herself with the sheets. Even in the morning light, she radiated an effortless beauty that left me in awe. "I hope you slept well, my lady," I greeted her with a smile.

"Very well, sir," she replied, also smiling.

As I headed to the kitchen to start the coffee, it dawned on me that I was still naked. But in my state of comfort and familiarity with Marci, it didn't faze me at all. After starting the coffee, I searched for some breakfast options and found a box of cakes. When Marci entered the kitchen, I offered her a cup of strong coffee and asked if she wanted anything else in it. Without hesitation, she took a sip and declared it perfect as it was.

I watched as she lit a cigarette and took a drag, entranced by the sensual grace with which she handled it. When she finished her smoke, she asked if it was okay to smoke inside again. And though it wasn't something I typically allowed in my apartment, there was something undeniably alluring about watching her indulge in such a simple pleasure.

"Of course, please make yourself at home," I responded.

After she finished her coffee, I asked if she would like to continue with her story. She agreed and I listened intently as she recounted the decline of her sex life and how her husband, Bill, blamed himself for it all.

Bill's inner turmoil about his sexual performance and size compared to other men had always been a source of insecurity for him. In his mind, he believed that most men were better equipped for sex than he was, causing him to constantly seek reassurance from his partner. Despite her constant attempts to ease his worries and assure him that size did not matter, Bill couldn't shake off his insecurities. As time went on, their intimate moments became less frequent, dwindling to only a few times a month. And even then, it was only because she didn't want to hear him beg for it anymore. Eventually, he stopped asking altogether but began making passive-aggressive comments about how she should find another lover who could satisfy her.

At first, she wasn't sure if he was just trying to get confirmation of her infidelity or if he was serious about finding someone else for her. But the idea of bringing another man into their marriage was not something she wanted. In fact, she wasn't even sure if she wanted to stay with Bill anymore. Then one day, she noticed that he would leave his computer open and unlocked whenever he went out of the room. It was no coincidence that every time she went into the study to get something from the desk, she would see the sites he had been visiting.

They all featured cuckolding and strong women dominating weak and sissy husbands. The more she saw, the more disgusted she became with the idea. After all, what woman would want a weak, pathetic man in her life? If that's how Bill saw himself, then maybe it was time for them to go their separate ways.

It wasn't until a year later that things between them reached a breaking point. They were hardly speaking to each other and slept in separate bedrooms. Their only interaction was at dinnertime, and even then it was strained and sporadic. Most nights, she would eat at the kitchen table while Bill ate in front of the TV. Their marriage had become nothing but a facade at that point.

That was when Bill brought an old high school friend home one night. The man was the epitome of attractiveness and masculinity, with bulging muscles that she couldn't take her eyes off of. It was clear why he was there, but even so, her hormones were on edge after not having sex for over a year. At that moment, it seemed like Bill's wish was about to come true.

But things didn't go as planned. Bill had intended to feign being drunk and leave them alone, but he played the part a little too well and ended up passing out in the guest bedroom upstairs. That left Larry and his wife alone downstairs, where they bonded over shared interests and were attracted to each other physically. Despite feeling guilty, she couldn't resist Larry's charm and found herself drawn to him more and more as the night went on. The tension between them finally reached its peak and she gave into her desires, knowing that their actions would have consequences for her marriage. But in that moment, she couldn't bring herself to care as Larry became the answer to all of her fantasies.

Despite being exhausted, Larry and I found ourselves back at my house, both knowing that we had nowhere else to go. And when he suggested sleeping on the couch, I couldn't help but feel a surge of anger towards Bill, who had put us in this situation. But as much as I wanted to punish Bill, I also couldn't deny the growing attraction between Larry and me.

Without fully comprehending my actions, I led Larry upstairs to my bedroom, ignoring his hesitant protests. He quickly gave in to my advances and soon we were tangled in the sheets, our bodies consumed with lust for each other.

But as the night went on and Larry thrust himself into every part of me, I couldn't help but feel guilty for betraying Bill. Yet at the same time, a sense of empowerment washed over me as I reveled in the pleasure that Larry brought me.

The next morning was even more confusing as we sat downstairs with Bill, who looked like a wreck after waking up alone. We didn't bother hiding our disheveled appearances or the fact that we had been intimate together all night long. And Bill's reaction was not what I had expected - instead of jealousy or anger, he seemed almost disappointed and betrayed.

I couldn't believe it - this was what he had wanted all along. To be a cuckold? But then why did he look so hurt? And why did I feel so torn between guilt and satisfaction? It was a conflicting mix of emotions that left me unsure of how to move forward from this messy situation.

The sound of Bill's voice echoed through the room, dripping with venom and hatred. He lunged towards me, his hand raised as if to strike. Before I could even flinch, Larry appeared out of nowhere and knocked Bill to the floor in one swift movement. The impact of his body hitting the ground made a loud thud and my heart raced with adrenaline.

Larry stood over Bill, placing his foot on his chest as a warning for him to stay down. I couldn't help but admire Larry's strength and quick reflexes. Part of me wanted to see Bill try to get up so that Larry could put him back in his place.

But then I did something that perhaps wasn't the wisest decision - I walked over to Bill and taunted him, lifting my robe to reveal my swollen and bruised privates. I knew it would only further enrage him, but at that moment, I didn't care.

Larry was caught off guard by my actions and before he could stop me, Bill had risen from the ground and struck me across the face. It was like a slap woke me up from a daze and I realized what I had done.

But before I could process my thoughts any further, Larry was on top of Bill, delivering swift punches and kicks. It was a chaotic mess, but I couldn't look away - there was something strangely exhilarating about watching two men fight over me.

Once Larry had made sure that Bill wouldn't cause any more harm, he left in a hurry, leaving me alone with my thoughts. At that moment, I didn't know who to root for - the man who treated me terribly or the one who fought for me.

After taking a shower and changing into comfortable clothes, I decided to leave the apartment for the day. I needed some time alone to think about everything that had happened. But as much as I tried to distract myself with shopping and a movie, my mind kept going back to Larry and what he must think of me.

Was Bill gone when you returned home?" I asked her.

"No, he was in the kitchen, putting the finishing touches on dinner. When I walked in and sat my purse down on the counter, he walked over and hugged me and told me to have a seat, and he would serve me my food. He acted like nothing happened even though the two black eyes told a different story. I had no idea what to do, so I did as he directed. I took a seat and allowed him to dish up the food and put it in front of me, along with a glass of wine. I was almost afraid to eat it, though, as I figured he might have poisoned it. He saw my hesitation reached over with his fork and took a bite from my plate. 'See it is safe to eat.' He said.

So we sat and ate in relative silence. I have to admit that he did a good job with the food. I had never seen him cook before except for a barbecue. I waited for him to bring up what had happened that morning, and he finally did but only to apologize to me for his behavior. 'I deserved what I got from Larry.' He told me. 'I thought that I would be able to accept my wife being with another man. All those websites make it sound so simple and so exciting. They don't tell you that there is a big difference between fantasy and reality. While we were all together last night before I got drunk, everything was going along the way I understood it should. I was getting excited thinking about how wonderful it would be to watch another man with my wife. And then when I woke up and figured out that it had happened without me even being awake to watch, I lost it. I should never have started this whole mess. I hope you can forgive me.'

She hesitated at that point and reached for her pack of cigarettes. She tamped one out a half inch grabbed it between her fingers, slid it out, and put it between her lips. It is the damnedest thing, but my cock started getting hard just watching her. She saw me staring at her, and she held the pack out in an invitation to me. "Go ahead, take one, I know you are dying to." At that point, the only thing I could think of was Satan tempting Eve with the apple, grape, pomegranate, or whatever fruit it was. And just like Eve, I succumbed to the temptation. I took one, put it between my lips, and lit it with her lighter. I saw her smile as I took that first drag and a little more when I started to become light-headed as the nicotine hit my system. Her brand was one with menthol in it, and it tasted wonderful. I sucked another big drag of smoke and pulled it as deep into my lungs as I could hold it there, to get the full impact. I knew that I was in danger of becoming hooked again on things, but I did not care. I loved how it made me feel. I think Marcie knew that I might become addicted to the cigarettes again, and as soon as I put the first one out, she handed me another. I started to wave it away, but she insisted. "If you want me to continue with this story, the least you can do is join me when I smoke." And right there, I knew that she was the devil in disguise.

As I finally emerged from the dizzying fog of nicotine, I eagerly implored her to continue her story. "So, did you forgive him?" I asked, my curiosity piqued.

She hesitated for a moment before answering. "I told him that he would have to earn my forgiveness," she said resolutely. "If he wanted to get back in my good graces, then he would have to show me that he was ready to accept what happened between Larry and me."

I raised an eyebrow at her bold ultimatum. "How is he supposed to do that? Do you want him to call Larry up and ask him to come back?"

She shook her head firmly. "No, I told him to get down on his knees and lick my cunt knowing full well that another man has dumped his load in it." Her words were sharp, full of anger and hurt.

I could see the conflict raging within her as she recounted this painful memory. But she went on, her voice growing colder as she spoke. "Well, his face got all red and I thought he was going to pop a blood vessel. But after a few minutes, he did as I asked. He got down on his knees right there in the kitchen, pulled off my shorts and underpants, and put his head between my thighs."

A shiver ran down my spine as I imagined this scene unfolding before me. She continued, "He took quite a long time smelling and tasting, probably checking for any remnants of his friend's cum left on or in me. But then he got serious about the whole thing and dived in with gusto."

Her breath hitched as she recalled the intensity of the moment. "I got excited real quick and pulled his head hard against my wet cunt, holding him there," she paused, a hint of satisfaction creeping into her tone. "He used everything he had that could make contact with my slit, including the tip of his nose. I kept him there until I had come down from a massive orgasm, almost as good as the one Larry had given me the night before."

I could sense the conflicting emotions swirling within her as she remembered this pivotal moment in her marriage. "I figured at that point, if Bill was willing to be my cunt lapper, I might be able to salvage what seemed like a lost marriage."

"Did that happen?" I asked, still trying to process everything she had just revealed.

She shook her head sadly. "No, it didn't. As you can see," she gestured towards the half-pack of cigarettes on the table between us, "things only got worse from there."

"I can tell there's so much more to this story," I said, feeling a sudden urgency to unravel all of its complexities.

She sighed and looked at her watch. "Unfortunately, I don't have time to tell it all today. I have things I need to accomplish and another meeting this evening." She paused for a moment before adding, "Why don't you come to the meeting tonight? Maybe we can get together afterward and continue this conversation."

I eagerly agreed, and she gathered her things to leave. Just before walking out the door, she turned around and flipped the half-pack of cigarettes my way. "Enjoy," she said with a hint of bitterness before exiting and closing the door behind

Chapter Five -Harold's Heartbreak: A Cuckold's Confession

The following day, I immersed myself in the arduous task of transcribing my recordings from the previous day. The air was thick with the tense energy of unfinished stories waiting to be told. After spending hours hunched over my notepad, I decided to change into more comfortable clothes and return to the meeting site.

As I re-entered the room, I couldn't help but notice the stark contrast from the night before - there were significantly fewer empty chairs and a palpable tension hung in the air. In the far back corner, I spotted Marcie once again, this time flanked by two other women. My mind raced with questions about how this development would be received by Bill and if it would cause any trouble.

My thoughts were quickly answered as Bill stormed into the room, his complexion turning from pink to white to an angry beet red. He made his way through the aisles towards Marcie's group, his body visibly shaking with anger. For a moment, I feared he may have a weapon concealed on him and that Marcie and her companions were in grave danger.

"What in the hell do you think you're doing?" Bill bellowed at Marcie. "It's bad enough that you came here alone to stir up trouble, but now you've brought more of your kind with you. I'm going to have to ask all three of you to leave immediately."

One of the women sitting beside Marcie spoke up without hesitation. "You and what army?" she challenged. "I've heard all about your supposed physical prowess, and if you're no better with your fists than you are with your words, I have no doubt any one of us could take you down."

Bill's face turned a dangerous shade of crimson as he clenched and unclenched his fists. I held my breath, afraid he might strike one of the women. But then I cleared my throat, signaling that I was watching. He turned to me and slowly released his fists, seeming to have trouble meeting my gaze. Eventually, he backed away from the confrontation, and the tension in the room began to dissipate.

Feeling a sense of relief wash over me, I settled back into my seat and tried to distract myself by observing the other individuals in the room. Among them was Fred, who had caught my attention with his honesty the night before. I hoped he would continue his story from where he left off - he seemed like the most genuine person in the group, and I was eager to hear more about his experiences.

The meeting began, and they all recited the serene serenity prayer. I joined in with an "amen" to fit in with the group. Bill gave me a lingering glance, and I prayed he wouldn't bring up my lack of contribution to the discussion. What could I add besides telling him what a foolish man he was for letting the most beautiful woman on earth slip away? Then I remembered her cruel streak and thought maybe he was smarter than me after all. Thankfully, he moved on and asked a newcomer if he would share his story.

The man's hand trembled as he hesitated, then with a deep breath, he stood and took the microphone. "My name is Harold," he said, his voice wavering. The room responded with the standard greeting of "Hi, Harold." And then he began his painful tale. Every word seemed to weigh heavily on his heart.

"I don't know if I can call myself a cuckold," Harold confessed, his eyes searching for understanding among the group. "But that's what you're expecting me to say, right?" He let out a bitter laugh before continuing. "All I know is that my wife is cheating on me with her boss." A collective gasp could be heard in the room. "It's been going on for a while, but I only found out for sure when I came home sick from work and caught them in our bed." Anger flickered in Harold's eyes. "Talk about disrespect, she didn't even have the decency to do it somewhere else."

"So, I did what any man would do," Harold continued, his voice shaking with emotion. "I raised hell. I told him to get the hell out of my house and never come back." His fists clenched at the memory. "And do you know what he did? He laughed at me." Tears threatened to spill from his eyes. "And my wife laughed right along with him."

Harold paused, taking a moment to regain his composure before continuing. "She grabbed his crotch and held it up for me to see and said, 'Which cock do you think I prefer? This big, fat one or your little, thin one?'" A mixture of disgust and pain filled his voice as he recounted the words. "Can you believe it?"

"Now here's your choice, Harold," his wife had said to him at that moment. "Either take off your clothes, sit in that chair, and jerk off while I finish screwing Malcolm, or get the fuck out of this house and don't come back until you're sure I'm not entertaining anyone. But if you stay, I expect you to clean up like a good little wimp." Harold's voice cracked as he finished the story.

The room fell silent, the weight of Harold's heart-wrenching experience hanging in the air. And yet, no one dared to ask what he decided. Perhaps they were too afraid to know the answer.

Feeling restless and unsatisfied by Harold's incomplete tale, Fred stood up and took the microphone. "Some of you have asked me to continue my tale of idiocy, so here goes." He paused, his eyes scanning the room. "Honestly, I'm surprised none of you know what I'm talking about. Haven't you read all the propaganda on the internet about cuckolding?"

Fred took a deep breath and began his own confession. "The conversation with my wife had been brewing in the back of my mind for weeks," he admitted. "And when she threw down her challenge, I couldn't resist." A sly smile tugged at his lips. "It was time to see if I could find a man who fit her criteria - muscular physique, rock-hard abs, and an impressively endowed cock."

A few chuckles could be heard around the room, but Fred's expression remained serious as he continued his tale. "Of course, the last one would be hard to determine without some sort of awkward measuring contest among men." A nervous laugh escaped his lips. "But I remained determined and turned to my immediate circle for potential candidates."

He recounted how he began dropping subtle hints to his wife about different men he thought she might like, showing her pictures here and there. But she remained steadfast in her demand for the perfect combination of attributes before even considering it.

The group sat in stunned silence as Fred finished his story. It was clear that these men had a lot to learn about relationships and the consequences of their actions.

It took me three months of relentless searching and convincing before I finally found someone who came close to the exact description I had conjured up for Marylyn. And another three months of pleading and promising before he agreed to go along with my seemingly insane scheme.

He was ready to call me crazy until I showed him a photo of my stunning wife, causing him to do a double-take. He demanded more revealing photos and luckily, I managed to secretly snap some while she was unaware. One particular photo, taken after she had just stepped out of the shower, sealed the deal for my chosen candidate. Her hair was wet and cascading down her back, and her breasts were perky and dripping with water droplets, making them even more alluring. There was no way any man could resist that sight.

With Tom on board, I arranged for him to come over and meet Marylyn at our house under the guise of an old friend visiting for dinner. Surprising her would only lead to disaster as she needed everything to be perfect - the house immaculate, a special meal prepared.

As we arrived at our doorstep, the mouthwatering aroma of delicious food greeted us. Tom remarked that this visit might be worth it after all. And then he caught sight of Marylyn and almost stumbled over his own words. She was playing the game to perfection. Her dress, made of sheer fabric, left nothing to the imagination and she wore no undergarments beneath it. To add to the seduction, her legs were adorned in six-inch heels, making them look even longer and sexier than usual. I had no idea she even owned those shoes - she had never worn them before in my presence.

"Is this what you had in mind, dear?" Marylyn purred as she greeted us at the door. "Or perhaps I am a little overdressed for our guest. Why don't you both have a seat while I dish up the food."

Truthfully, at that point, I had lost my appetite. The sight of Marylyn was both mesmerizing and infuriating - knowing that she was about to seduce another man right in front of me. But I couldn't back out now. As Tom eagerly devoured his meal, he couldn't help but shower my wife with compliments every few bites, causing her to blush and smile.

When it was clear that dinner was over, Marylyn turned to me and said, "Clean off the table and do the dishes while I get acquainted with your friend."

As I started clearing away the dishes, I could hear Marylyn's sultry voice leading Tom into the living room. My heart sank as I knew there was no stopping this train now. The jealousy within me burned hotter and hotter as I imagined what would happen next.

I rushed through my task, trying to balance speed and precision. I didn't want my wife to criticize my work in front of Tom, so I made sure every detail was perfect. When I was finally satisfied, I entered the living room and found my wife on Tom's lap. Her arms were tightly wrapped around his neck and her lips were pressed against his. One strap of her dress had slipped off her shoulder, revealing just a hint of her nipple. Tom's hand was boldly exploring the curve of her backside, and I could see the desire in both of their eyes.

My wife, Maryln, looked up at me with a mischievous grin. "Take a seat," she purred. "Now that our audience is here, let the show begin."

She disentangled herself from Tom's lap and took a few steps back. "Alright, Tom. Let's see if you meet our third criteria. Are you hung like a stallion?"

"I don't know about that, but I'm certainly big enough to satisfy you," Tom replied confidently.

"Well, let me see it for myself before I decide whether or not to let you have me," Maryln taunted.

Tom glanced over at me, seeking some sort of approval, but I could only sit there speechless. This was what I thought I wanted, but now that it was happening right in front of me, doubts flooded my mind.

But if I stopped it now, Maryln would never let me live it down. And if I didn't stop it, I wasn't sure I could live with myself. How foolish I must have seemed to everyone.

The room fell silent as we all waited for Fred to continue his story. He started to put down the microphone, but without thinking, I blurted out: "No way in hell, Fred! You need to tell us the whole story right now!"

Bill, one of our friends, stood up to scold me, but the rest of the group chimed in with their encouragement for Fred to continue.

"Alright, if you want to hear all the sordid details," Fred reluctantly began.

Tom slowly rose from his seat and unbuckled his belt with deliberate movements. He then unbuttoned his dress pants and slowly lowered the zipper. With a teasing smile, he pushed the slacks down off his hips and stepped out of them. Turning to face me, he spoke directly: "Pick up my clothes and fold them neatly."

I hesitated, feeling confused and humiliated. Tom hadn't even made me a cuckold yet, but he was already giving me orders. Just as I was about to argue or protest, Marylyn spoke up, her voice dripping with condescension: "Just do it, wimp. This is what you wanted, isn't it? Might as well participate."

I got up from my chair walked over and did as he told me. When he was satisfied that I would comply with his requests, he told me to lower his shorts for him. Again I hesitated, but it only took one look from Marylyn to let me know that I better obey. So I hooked my fingers into each side of his shorts and pulled them down. He did not attempt to step out of them, though, as he pointed towards his feet and told me to get down on my knees and remove his underpants for him. I heard my wife gasp as I obeyed, and I looked up to see the largest cock I had ever seen in my life standing straight up and proud away from Tom's hips.

'As long as you're in the position, you might as well give Tom's cock a little kiss. You do want a little taste of the monster cock that is going to go in my cunt in a few minutes, don't you?'

I could not believe how fast my wife had gotten into the dominant mood once she had made up her mind to follow through. And Tom was playing right along with her as he turned so that his cock was in front of my face and grabbed my hair and pulled me to him. 'Lick it wimp.' he demanded, and with his free hand, he pushed the tip of his cock against my lips.

I kept my lips tightly shut, refusing to go that far, but I was no match physically or even mentally for Tom. He looked at my wife and asked her how far she wanted him to push me, and her answer was, 'All the way.' And so he pulled my head back and with his other hand bitch slapped me. My wife cheered and told him to do it again, which he did. "Now, stick out your tongue and start licking, or things are going to become bad quick for you."

I didn't have much choice so I stuck out my tongue and began licking all around the head of his cock..

"Put it in his mouth so that he can see how far it is going to go inside of me," my wife urged.

"Open up, wimp," Tom demanded with a sneer.

Slowly, unwillingly, I parted my lips and allowed his hard member to invade my mouth. The thick shaft slid in easily at first, but as it reached the back of my throat, I gagged and choked. Marylyn had warned me not to vomit, knowing that Tom would follow through on his threats of violence if I did. So I forced myself to keep still as he plunged deeper into my mouth.

But then, to my surprise, he pulled out and walked over to the bed where Marylyn lay waiting for him. She was propped up on her elbows, her eyes wide with excitement and anticipation.

"Get your ass over here, cocksucker. Tom needs your assistance," she shouted eagerly.

I hesitated, unsure of what exactly she meant by "assistance". But one look at her determined expression told me that disobeying was not an option. With trembling legs, I made my way over to them.

Marylyn was lying on her back with her knees bent and spread wide open. Tom hovered over her, supporting himself with his hands and feet as he positioned himself between her legs.

"Guide his cock into my cunt," Marylyn demanded breathlessly.

My heart sank as I realized what she was asking of me. I couldn't believe she wanted me to assist another man in penetrating her. But before I could protest or even process what was happening, Tom was already lowering himself towards her awaiting entrance.

I grasped his member at the base and angled it towards her opening. As soon as the tip touched her slick folds, she let out a loud moan and began gushing with arousal. And just like that, he thrust himself all the way inside of her.

It didn't take long for me to realize that Tom wasn't wearing a condom. My stomach twisted in knots at the thought of him riding my wife bareback, but it was too late to say anything. I stepped back and watched in a daze as he moved inside her, their bodies slick with sweat and their moans filling the room.

I couldn't help but feel a pang of jealousy as I watched my wife experience pleasure that I had never been able to give her. My heart broke at the realization that I could never take her to the heights of ecstasy that this stranger could.

It seemed like they were locked in a passionate embrace for hours, though in reality, it was probably only minutes. And through misty eyes, I listened to the grunts and moans of two people lost in passion.

When they finally finished, I wiped away my tears and saw something even worse than watching them have sex. They were lying together, side by side, his arm draped over her protectively as he gently kissed her mouth. They were completely lost in each other, no longer putting on a show for me but truly enjoying each other's company.

And in that moment, I knew that my wife was lost to me forever.

As Fred finished his story and put down the microphone, he slowly made his way toward the doorway of the room. My heart felt heavy as I watched him leave. I wanted to yell at him to come back, to continue sharing his tale. There was still so much more that needed to be told, but I was too moved by his heartbreaking words to form any coherent thoughts.

The room fell into a heavy silence as nobody stepped up to take Fred's place. Even Bill, who always had a story to tell, remained silent. It seemed like everyone in that room was processing what they had just heard. I could see in their eyes that some of them saw themselves in Fred's tragic story.

I knew that no one else would share a story that evening that could rival what Fred had just told us. Feeling overwhelmed, I stood up and made my way towards the door. As I left the meeting room and stepped out into the parking lot, I reached into my shirt pocket and pulled out Marcie's cigarettes. Lighting one up, I took slow drags and let the smoke calm my nerves. I couldn't stop thinking about Fred and wishing I could hear the rest of his story. People deserve to know the truth about what happens when a man becomes a cuckold.

But as I leaned against my car door, finishing my cigarette, I knew that Fred was long gone and most likely wouldn't return for another meeting. He had shared everything he had to give, bearing his soul for all of us to see. Like a widower who has shed all his tears, there was nothing left for him.

Suddenly, the clicking of high heels cut through the quiet night air. Looking up, I saw not only Marcie approaching but her two female friends as well.

"Good evening, Jack," Marcie greeted me with a smile. "I thought you might like to meet a couple of my good friends. Jack, this is Helen. Her husband also convinced her to live the cuckold lifestyle, and this lady is Marylyn."

I was so stunned I could have almost stepped on my tongue. It was hard for me to believe that Fred had shared such intimate details not only in front of a group of men but also in front of his ex-wife.

There was a pause as I tried to process this new information until Marcie snapped her fingers in front of my face. "Snap out of it, Jack. If you want to hear the rest of the story, you better invite us back to your place where we can drink, smoke, and talk."

With a surge of excitement, I eagerly agreed and led them to my car.

Chapter Six – Confessions in the Group

The three women all sat on my sofa and waited as I fixed their drinks. I was glad that they were not too picky about their alcohol because I had not stopped to replenish my liquor supply. By the time I had returned with their drinks, the living room was blue with the smoke from their cigarettes, and I began to wonder if smoking and cuckolding went hand in hand.

I took a seat in one of my armchairs and waited patiently for someone to begin to tell their story. Marylyn was the first to stub out her cigarette and look me in the eyes. "Marcie told me that you are a reporter of some kind, looking for a story. Why this story, and why this particular group?"

"As I told Marcie, this is a follow-up on a story I did about a suicide. That investigation led me to the cuckold lifestyle and eventually to this group. Everything that I had read or seen before this group made it sound like the men all fell in love with the idea of their wives sleeping with other men. But then I came across one man who hated the idea so much that he took his own life, and it got me thinking that maybe someone needed to tell a different story. From the bits and pieces I have picked up at the meetings, I am concluding that maybe cuckolding isn't as well received by men as we have been led to believe."

"The only part of the story that these Internet sites have got right is that most of the time, the idea is brought up by the husband. Very few wives look for another man to bring home to their beds. Oh, sure, a lot of wives cheat, but that is a whole different thing. Usually, they try to hide their affairs from their men, not rub them in their faces. But when a man pushes his wife to do something that is, in fact, abhorrent to her long enough, she may react in a way he did not expect." And then Marylyn took a breath and a drink of whiskey before continuing with her story.

"I have to hand it to Fred. At least, he told the truth when he said he was at these meetings because he was a damned fool. I would have never cheated on him regardless of how bad our sex life was if he hadn't shoved another man down my throat. He just wouldn't let the idea go away. Every time I turned around, he was making some suggestions about how much I needed to feel a new and bigger cock inside me. At some point, I began to like the idea. I had become so disgusted with Fred and his constant harping that I no longer enjoyed sex with him. And I do have a healthy libido.

When Fred called that afternoon and said he was bringing home a friend, I knew that he was bringing the friend for me. By that time, I was ready for a cock inside me, so I dressed like a whore and allowed Tom to use me like a whore. But somewhere between forcing Fred to feed Tom's cock into my cunt and having three mind-numbing orgasms, I went from whore to lover for Tom. And I knew he felt the same way when he rolled off of me and did not get out of bed but pulled me to him and began kissing me gently and sweetly.

I didn't even notice that Fred had left the room. I was the most contented I had been in years, and I just snuggled against a man that I had known for less than two hours and went into the most peaceful sleep I could remember. And Tom must have felt pretty good about the situation himself because when I awoke the next morning, he still had me held in his arms.

He awoke when I tried to extricate myself from him looked into my eyes and smiled at me. Without worrying about morning breath, he pulled me to him and began kissing me with such urgency that I was almost instantly wet and wanting him inside me again. We made love slowly exploring each other bodies really for the first time. The previous night had been all about passion, but the morning was all about getting comfortable with each other. It was a learning experience for each of us to find out exactly what buttons to push to bring the other greater pleasure. I know you will not believe it, but I fell in love with Tom in those blessed few minutes."

"There must be more to the story than that. Fred intimated that he had gone through some other humiliating experiences at your and Tom's hands."

"There is always more to the story than people want to tell. I can say that I would have been happy to end my marriage that very morning but, of course, that wasn't a reasonable expectation. Tom and I were sitting enjoying a cup of coffee when Fred walked into the room. He could not even bring himself to look me in the eye, but I could tell he was beyond pissed from the redness of his face and the veins popping out on his forehead. He poured himself some coffee and slammed the mug down onto the counter. I ignored the tantrum, but Tom did not. He got up from the chair and walked towards Fred until he was right up, almost touching his chest. 'I am going to tell you this just once, and I hope you are smart enough to listen. You are the one that brought me into this house and your wife's bed. If you are angry with anyone, it should be you for being so stupid. Now I want you to take your coffee into another room and drink it quietly while you calm down. If you make any more of a scene, things are going to turn out bad for you.' Fred apparently got the implication, and although his face was still red, he picked up his mug and took his leave.

Tom then turned to me and asked me if I wanted him to leave. I emphatically told him, no, and then like a teenage girl, I blurted out that I loved him. He looked me deep in the eyes and brought his lips to mine. It was not a kiss of passion but rather a kiss of possession. 'I love you too.' he told me, and I was the happiest I had been in years.

I couldn't wait to tell someone about my good fortune, and so I told the only other person in the house. I walked in and told Fred that he needed to get his stuff out of my bedroom because Tom would be moving in. He broke down and started crying, and a strange thing happened to me. As I watched the tears roll down his face, I did not feel sorry for him. I felt contempt and maybe even a little bit of hatred towards him, and I vowed that I would see tears in his eyes, every chance I got.

I know that you must think me a monster."

I did not know how to answer her. I figured that there had been a lot going on between the times that he first broached the subject until the time he brought Tom home with him

"I imagine that this all didn't happen at that very moment, but rather some of your negative feelings were building up over time," I said.

"Truthfully, I think I began to lose respect for him the first time he brought up the idea of me sleeping with another man. I won't attempt to speak for all women, but as for me, I could never respect a man who viewed himself so negatively that he would want some other man to perform in his stead. The more he pushed the idea onto me, the more I despised him. And once I took the final step and bedded another man, my marriage was all but over. As for me, I would have thrown Fred and his clothes out the door that very moment, but Tom had other ideas, and the more I listened to him, the more I liked them. Tom told me that he had a sadistic streak, and he would like to spend time tormenting Fred if I didn't mind. And you know what, I relished the idea. I wanted the man that threw me away to suffer, and I made up my mind to not just sit back and watch but to partake of the festivities myself."

She again took a break from the story and held out her empty glass to me. As I took it, she was lighting a cigarette and allowing the smoke and nicotine to invade her body, bringing a calmness to her. When I walked back into the room, balancing four drinks and not just one, I noticed that the other two women were sitting closer together on the sofa. Marcie had her arm around Helen's shoulders, and Helen had one arm tucked around Marcie's waist. Helen's lips were slightly puffed out, and I wondered if they had been kissing while I was out of the room. Marcie caught me staring and then let out a little laugh. "What is the matter, Jack? Haven't you ever wanted to watch a little girl-on-girl action?"

I thought to myself that yes, I had, but I did not utter those words. I just said. "If you ladies would like a little privacy, I don't mind if you use my bed while I hear the rest of Marylyn's story."

"To hell with that idea," Marylyn interjected. "If there is going to be a girl-on-girl action, I am going to be right in the middle of it."

"Well, how about it, Jack? Would you like to join three smoking hot women in your bed?"

I looked at her and cocked my head to see if she was serious. This could be a dream come true for some men, but a man has to know his limitations. "I figure I am man enough to hold my own with one of you, and I might even be able to make a fair showing with two of you, but I don't think there is a man alive that could handle all three."

"Don't worry; I have a way to keep your cock hard until we are ready for you to cum. If you're game, that is."

I didn't think that I would ever get a chance like this again, and so I agreed. The women rose as one and grabbed me by the arm. Since Marcie already knew the way she led the group we were soon all huddled around the bed. Helen was the first to begin removing her clothes, and I watched with rapt attention. I thought that Marcie was as good a looking naked woman as I had ever seen, but Helen was in the same classification. Her body was solid with not an ounce of fat on it. Her breasts had no sag to them but jutted out and up with her nipples, almost sticking towards the ceiling. Her waist was tiny, and her hips flared out just the right amount to catch the eye and hold it there. Her legs were long and firm, and even if she had not been wearing heels, they would have enticed a man to want to feel them wrapped around his waist. She shook her head, and her honey-blonde curls settled down and framed a perfect face. She wore just a hint of lipstick, but anyone would have been drawn to that succulent opening in her face.

I had been so engrossed in watching her that I didn't even realize that two other naked women were in the room. But then Marcie brought me out of my dream-like state.

"You are way behind in the undressing department. Come on, get out of those dubs, and get ready for some action."Of course, I obeyed, but by the time I was completely undressed, Helen and Marylyn were already entwined with each other on the bed. Only Marcie had not joined in the fun as she waited patiently for me. As my shorts hit the floor, she stepped up and said. "Now for the surprise. Put your hands behind your back."

I did as she requested, although I felt a little spark of fear in the pit of my stomach. That fear grew to a minor panic as I felt her snapping steel rings around my wrists. She left me standing there with my arms restrained and disappeared from the room. When she came back, she was lugging a tall kitchen stool with her, which she sat down a little way from the foot of the bed. "Climb aboard cowboy," she said as she grabbed my elbow and led me to the stool. I know what you are thinking why in the world would I agree to such a thing? But then you have never had the opportunity to watch three of the most beautiful women in the world put on a show for you. Or maybe you have, I only know that I had not. So I let her maneuver me into the position she wanted. When I was seated, she reached down and grabbed one of my ankles brought it as far back as possible, and secured it with my foot stuck around the metal ring that circled the stool. Then she repeated the action with my other leg, and now I was quite uncomfortable with a lot of pressure on my legs. I tried bending forward to take the pressure off of them, but Marcie quickly put an end to that as she shoved my shoulders back against the tall backing of the stool and wrapped a cord around me holding me in that position.

"And now, as I promised, I will make sure you stay hard until we need your cock." She produced two metal rings, one about twice as big around as the other. Taking one of my testicles between her fingers, she began pushing it through the larger ring. When it was completely through, she forced the other testicle through behind it. "And now for your cock. My, it really won't go through being that hard. I will have to do something to soften it up." She took my balls between her sharp fingernails and began to squeeze them until the pain was severe enough that I was begging her to stop. But she did not relent until I was soft enough for her to bend my cock in two and insert it through the ring as well. Before I could get hard again, she pushed the smaller ring over the head of my cock and down to its very base. She bent towards me brought her lips to mine and forced her tongue into my mouth. I could feel my cock beginning to harden as she squeezed it with her fingers. The two actions brought me back rock-hard within seconds.

And then I felt pain as the tender flesh of my cock began to swell out against the unrelenting steel of that second ring. In just seconds, the first ring that was behind my ball sacks was putting pressure onto the cords that held my testicles to my body. Blood was rushing into my cock, but it became trapped there, unable to flow back out. The more blood that came in, the harder I got, and the harder I got, the more blood was trapped. There was no way that I would be able to lose this painful erection without some type of help. And since I was tied in place and the women were busy with each other, I didn't expect to get help anytime soon. I began to worry about how long a man could stay hard without damage being done to his sex organs. I had heard the commercials for ED medication that said if you have an erection for more than four hours to call a physician, but I did not know if that applied to a forced erection. And so I did the only thing that made sense. I screamed.

I have no idea how Marcie disentangled herself so quickly, but like a flash, she was in front of me, forcing my mouth to open and shoving what I figured was one of their panties into it. "That was a very naughty thing to do. Now, if one of your neighbors calls the police, we will be forced to lie to them and make them believe that it was one of us in the throes of passion. But before that happens, I am going to have to teach you a lesson in obedience." She walked over to my pants and pulled my belt from the loops. She bent it in half and made a show of snapping it together.

The other two women were sitting up in anticipation as Marcie walked back to me. She raised the belt over her head and brought it down smartly on the top of my shoulders first one side and then the other. She then moved lower and brought the leather across both of my nipples at once. The pain flared outward from them and seemed to travel to all my extremities. I would have screamed, but the wadded-up panties prevented that from happening. She continued with her discipline until I had tears running down my cheeks. That seemed to calm her, and she reached out and patted me on the side of my face.

"Now, now. That is so much better. Please don't make me angry again. I have tits, cunts, and mouths to attend to. And she joined the others back on the bed."

I would have sworn that the pain from her whipping would have caused me to lose my erection, but if it went down at all, it again regained its swelling as I watched the women return to their orgy on my bed. It was hard to keep track of who was pleasuring who because they seemed to be almost one six-legged, six-armed monster. They were rolled into a very large ball, with Helen's head stuck between Marcie's thighs, Marcie's head stuck between Marylyn's thighs, and Marylyn's head stuck between Helen's thighs. All I could hear was sucking and lapping sounds as three tongues and mouths worked three cunts. And of course, I was both in agony and ecstasy at the same time.

The whole mass of arms and legs were writhing against each other, and they were all moaning although much muted from the position of their mouths. Almost simultaneously, their bodies began to spasm, and they ground even harder together until finally, they came to rest and separated from each other.

They all got up and came and stood around my stool. I was in terrible pain by that time, not only from my cock but also from the fact that my legs had cramped. Helen looked down at my cock and reached out and gently touched it. But even that gentle feel caused more pain to radiate into my gut.

"My isn't that just a wonderful shade of purple? And it is so cold as well. I think it might be nice to feel that inside my cunt."

"Let's get him off the stool then and onto the bed."

They all worked together, freeing my legs and feet. I could not hold myself upright as they helped me off the stool, but the three of them working together managed to get me across the room and lay flat on my back. Two of them began to massage the knots out of my legs as Helen straddled my hips and guided my cold sore cock into her very warm wet snatch. She let out a little whimper of joy as she settled down all the way until her pelvic bone was against my pubic hair. Then she began to rock side to side and back and forth but not up and down. I could feel her muscles squeezing me, and I knew she had been doing some kind of weird exercise. If I had not been in such severe pain, I would have probably been in seventh heaven. Then she began to rise and settle back down. With each stroke, she would pull almost off of me and then plunge back down with a vengeance. When she had my cock as deep inside her as it would go, she would grind her body against mine, causing me even more pain. I tried to tighten my hips in the hopes of bringing me off, but it was to no avail. The pain was so great that my mind could not fathom allowing me to ejaculate. I don't know how long that went on before I finally felt her begin to throb, and she threw her head back and let out a scream almost as loud as the one I had made when I was crying for help. And then she was still looking down at me with an expression that I could not read. I wanted to think that it was a look of compassion, but it might just as well have been one of loathing.

She climbed off of me and motioned for Marylyn to take her place, which she did. Before sliding it into her tunnel, she reached down and squeezed my cock at its base as if she thought she needed to bring it to a firmer state. "I love the icy feel of that," she said, and then she settled down and began using me as if I was a cold dildo. Tears were again streaming down my face, caused by not only the pain but also the anxiety of the damage that might be done to my poor cock. She did not let my tears deter her. She took her time enjoying the ride bringing her to the brink and then resting before beginning to build towards orgasm once more. As if I needed more pain, she reached down and began pinching my nipples between her long fingernails. Just when I thought that she would cut them clean from my body, she would twist them from side to side, which would force my hips off the bed and drive my sore cock deeper into her cunt. And of course, that made her want to twist my nipples some more. Finally and mercifully, she began to tighten her hips and allowed herself to violently begin to shake. I looked up and saw that she was biting her lower lip to keep from screaming out and waking the dead. And then it was over, and she too slid off of my body, but she did not get off the bed. Instead, she settled herself over the top of my face, removed the panties from behind my teeth, and brought her cunt down onto my mouth. "Lick it and be glad you didn't cum inside me."

She was wet and musky, but I allowed my tongue to flick out of my mouth and do a little dance up the length of her folds. I found her taste to be pleasant and had just stuck my tongue deep inside of her when I felt someone pulling roughly on the metal ring surrounding my cock. Involuntarily my hips came off the bed to relieve the pressure, but they could only rise so far. And then I felt the ring slip a little bit and then a little more until with a rush it came all the way off. For just a moment, the pain was worse than it was when the ring was in place as new blood began to circulate. But I still did not lose my erection as yet another cunt engulfed me inside of it.

"Mmm, he is beginning to warm up. I really should have left the ring on for at least part of the ride. Oh well, perhaps another time, and Marcie began to slow fuck me. But now I was beginning to gain pleasurable feelings in my cock. My balls had been building over time, and I knew that once they let loose, I would fill Marcie to overflowing. And then I remembered Marylyn's warning about not ejaculating. For me, however, it was far too late for that. I was going to cum and cum hard.

Marcie felt me tensing up and immediately rose up and off of my body. "You naughty boy, you were trying to release your load inside of me without my permission. That simply is not allowed."

Of course, even without further stimulation, I began to spasm. I was sure that without a receptacle, my cum would splatter onto the ceiling, but I had another surprise. Because of the ring surrounding my cock and balls, there still was too much pressure to allow my cum to jet out of my body. Instead, it came out in little slow trickles, and my satisfaction level was restricted as well. As little drops of cum dripped from the head of my cock, all three women were roaring with laughter.

"I love to see a male frustrated," Marcie announced. "Maybe next time we should just milk him."

"And miss the feel of his Popsicle?" Helen laughed. "I don't think so. The trick will be to get him to agree to a repeat performance."

"I knew that we should have taken some pictures." Announced Marylyn. "We could have used them as leverage to get him to agree to another round."

And again, they burst out in laughter.

They watched for just a few minutes to see how much ejaculate would pool onto my belly and then began to get dressed. I was pissed, but with my hands tied behind my back, I thought better of making too big a scene. Marcie was the last one ready to leave, and as she headed for the door, she turned and tossed the handcuff keys in my direction. They landed on the floor beside the bed, so it took me some time to retrieve them and unlock the cuffs. By that time, Marcie had blown me a kiss and closed the door behind her.

Chapter Seven - An Unpleasant Surprise

I needed to get cleaned up and assess the damage. However, my heart was racing, and I chose to light a cigarette and sit down in the living room to smoke it. I knew that I was once again hooked on nicotine and wondered how much pain and suffering I would go through this time to break the habit. I knew one thing for sure; I would not be attempting withdrawal symptoms until I had finished the investigative work on this piece of journalism.

I had smoked the cigarette down to the filter and jabbed the last spark out in the ashtray. I got up and made my way into the bathroom and turned on the brightest lights and then the shower. I stepped to where I had the most light and inspected my cock and balls. The first thing I had to do was remove the larger ring that still encompassed my penis and testicles. I tried pulling one of my testicles back through the ring but to no avail. There just was not enough room to get it through. I hesitated for a moment thinking back to how Marcie had gotten all of this meat into such a constricted space, knowing that I would have to follow the steps in reverse to accomplish my mission. Then it struck me that the last thing to go into the ring had been my cock so it would have to be the first thing to come out.

I was completely flaccid by that time, so bending my penis in half to get the head pointed out of the ring was fairly simple. However, pushing it through was another matter. It wanted to bunch up instead of sliding out smoothly. All of the women's juices had dried and crusted by that time, and so there was no slippery moisture to aid me in my cause. I thought of various options, including cooking oil, but I was not sure I had any. Margarine sounded like it might work, but that too, I discounted. Finally, I turned on the shower adjusted it to lukewarm, and climbed in. Taking a bar of soap, I lathered my cock and the surrounding area and soon had it slipping out of the ring. That just left my two jewels to be freed.

There was enough room now, but it was still painful pushing against the ring. But with a little extra shove and a lot of extra pain, I had them free. I finished washing the rest of my body and then stepped out on the mat and dried myself off with my large terry towel. Only then did I get an opportunity to survey the damage those rings had done to my flesh.

I noticed two distinct, very ugly black and blue rings. One that went all the way around my cock near the base, although it was much darker and more painful on the top than it was on the softer underside. The second ring was right at the base of my cock, where the large ring had been pushed down as far as it would go before my pelvic bone had stopped it. I could not see behind my balls, so I did not know if that ring went all the way around, but I assumed it did.

My mind was racing, trying to figure out whether I should go to the emergency room and let them examine me, but that would have taken a much more secure man than me. So I hunted in the medicine cabinet and found some pain-removing cream and rubbed a generous amount into the wounded area. Within a few minutes, the pain started to let up, whether that was due to the cream or natural healing I had no idea.

I put on a terry robe and made my way back to the kitchen, where I fixed an extra-strong glass of bourbon and ginger ale. I drank it in about two gulps and fixed another before sitting down and reflecting on what had taken place. I was amazed at just how cruel those three women were, and I began to wonder if perhaps they were the ones telling the fabricated story. Maybe it was their idea to cuckold their husbands and to make them miserable. But then I remembered Fred's story, which seemed to collaborate what the women had said. But that was only one story among many others. I would have to return to the meeting and hope to find a way to interview one or two of the men.

I spent a restless night dreaming about beautiful women holding all types of sharp objects and removing male body parts with them. One dream was so vivid that I could swear my testicles were being severed from my body and tossed into a pan of boiling oil. As I watched from a bound position on a kitchen stool, three women removed the morsels and began cutting them into little pieces and then feeding them to each other. The look of rapture on their faces told me that these were delicacies that they had acquired a taste for. And then Marcie announced, "Well, that was nice, but now we need to cook his cock." And that is when I woke up drenched in sweat.

Chapter Eight - I Could Not Have Predicted This

The next evening I arrived at the meeting place earlier than usual. I parked again as far from the door as I could and waited for the men to arrive. I snapped pictures of each of their license plates for future lookups and pictures of the men so that I would remember which went with which cars. Bill was among the last to arrive, and before getting out of his car, he surveyed the other vehicles in the lot. His gaze fell directly on my car and then on me, sitting behind the wheel. With determination, he walked toward me, and I knew that he had something specific in mind as he came.

I turned to the open window as he bent down and placed a big hand on my arm. "I am not sure exactly what your game is, Jack if that is your real name. But I did not just fall off the turnip truck yesterday. You are not one of us, at least not in the same way that the rest of the men here are. And I watched you talking with Marci the other night and with all three of the female Nazis last night. So why don't you explain what your reason for being here is?"

"What makes you think that I am any different than any of the other men that come to your meetings? Perhaps, I am just not ready to spill my guts to the world."

"For one thing," he began. "You just gave yourself away right now when you referred to it as 'your meetings' and not our meetings. And for another thing, you pay way too much attention to the stories. Most of the men here don't need to hear the details. They have already lived most of them. You, on the other hand, not only listen avidly you insist that some of the men give even more detail than they intend to. I am thinking that you are either a reporter or some type of private investigator gathering dirt for a divorce hearing."

I didn't answer him, and so he turned and began walking back towards the building entrance. As he did, he took out his phone and made a call. I sat in my car, wondering whether it would be a good idea to go in and try to get a little more information. I was just about ready to get out of my vehicle when I noticed red and blue lights sweeping around my car. I looked in the mirror and saw that a metro police vehicle was directly behind me, and an officer was getting out and cautiously walking toward my side of the car. He had not removed his weapon, but his hand was held very close to the butt of the pistol, and the hammer strap had been pulled free.

"Put your hands on the wheel and remain in the vehicle," He ordered.

I complied and waited for him to shine his flashlight in my eyes. "Do you have any weapons in the vehicle?" He asked.

I responded that I did not and asked him why he was questioning me.

"We had a complaint that someone was harassing members of this group. It was alleged that this individual was in a car exactly like yours and that he had a gun in his possession. Would you mind stepping out of the vehicle so that my partner can search it?"

I thought about asking him if he had a warrant, but then what did I have to hide? I did not have anything in my car that was illegal or dangerous, so I cautiously opened the door and stepped out with my hands in plain view. "Be my guest," I stated.

The second policeman opened the passenger door and rummaged around in the glove box and the console before looking beneath the front seat. He then moved to the rear door and checked the seatbacks and beneath the backseat bench. Finally, he asked for my keys and opened the trunk. Within just a few seconds, he emerged with a small packet of white powder in his hand. "I guess you will have to come down to the station. You have the right to remain silent."

I did not hear the rest, as my mind was whirling a hundred miles per hour. I knew that I had been set up and that the packet had been planted there, but I did not know why. I was handcuffed and put in the back of the police cruiser. Neither cop spoke to me, nor did I try to speak to them.

When we arrived at the police station, I was helped out of the car and led inside to a small room where the cuffs were removed, and my fingerprints were taken as well as mug shots. It was then explained to me that I was to be arraigned in the morning on felony drug charges and that I was allowed one phone call before being placed in my cell.

I did not know whom to call, as I did not retain a lawyer. So I simply asked that a lawyer be assigned to me until I could retain counsel of my own. They told me that one would be assigned but that he probably would not show up until just before my hearing in the morning.

They led me to a cell. I was grateful that it was not the drunk tank and that there was no one else occupying it at present. I settled down on the bunk and held my head in my hands. I now realized that the phone call Bill had made was what set this whole chain of events in motion, and I wondered just how far he was willing to go to frame an innocent man.

I must have dozed off because I was startled when I heard my name called. I looked up to see a very professional-looking woman standing by the now-open cell door. "My name is Jennifer Byers. I have been retained to represent you in this matter. However, it now appears that there is no matter to represent you on. The packet the officer confiscated from your car contained plain old baking soda. Unfortunately, your camera got badly damaged somehow in the search, and your data card is missing."

"You said you had been retained on my behalf? Would you mind telling me who it was that called you?"

"I am only at liberty to say that she wishes to remain anonymous. Come on; I will help you get your belongings back and give you a ride back to your car."

I thought about asking her about filing charges for false arrest, but I was sure that would not go anywhere. I might be able to recover the cost of my camera in small claims court, but even that seemed like a wasted effort. "I suppose that I don't have much recourse against those that perpetrated this farce?" I asked.

"Oh, there are several different avenues you might take if you could prove who was responsible. But it would be very expensive as no lawyer would take it on for a contingency. My advice would be to let it drop for now, along with any investigation that you are considering continuing."

"And just how much do you know about my investigation?" I asked.

"I know that you have been hanging around the cuckold's anonymous meetings and that you have had contact with three wives of some very powerful men."

"Don't you mean ex-wives?" I responded.

"I have said more than I should have already. I will give you a word to the wise, however. Some people are willing to share certain things in a closed group, but they are not willing to share those things with the world, especially if their identities were revealed."

She pulled into the parking lot, and I thanked her before getting out of the car. She smiled at me and told me that she was well paid for her time. She made sure that I got into my vehicle and got the motor running before she proceeded to drive away.

I drove very carefully back to my apartment, keeping a close watch on my mirrors for any other cop cars that might be lurking there.

As I walked into my apartment, the weight of the day's events settled heavily on my shoulders. The betrayal, the deceit, and the lurking danger all swirled in my mind, leaving me feeling more vulnerable than ever. I poured myself a stiff drink and sank into the worn armchair by the window, staring out at the dimly lit city below.

Chapter Nine - Another Surprise

As I walked into my apartment, I checked my watch and noticed that it was nearly four in the morning. Without even brushing my teeth, I crawled into my bed and passed out from nervous exhaustion. Again I had violent dreams featuring beautiful but deadly women, and I awoke feeling, neither refreshed nor ready to face another day. I turned on my shower to as hot as I could stand it and let the water run over my neck and shoulders for a long time. Only when the temperature of the water dropped below scalding did I decide to lather up and then rinse off. I finished my normal morning routine and then went to the kitchen to make coffee.

I was just finishing my second cup when I heard someone gently rap on my front door. I adjusted my robe, making sure that it was securely closed, and then opened the door. To my surprise, both Fred and Marylyn stood on my stoop. "May we come in?" Fred asked.

I nodded and then stepped back and to the side, waving them inside with the sweep of my hand. I offered them coffee, which they accepted. I poured what was left in the pot into two cups and then made a second pot and started it to drip.

I waited until they had mixed their coffee and had taken a few sips before I spoke. "I have to say I am surprised to see both of you here. What do I owe the pleasure of your visit?"

Again I was surprised that it was Fred and not Marylyn that answered me. "We heard what happened at the meeting last night, and we came to offer our apologies."

"What do you have to apologize for? I am quite sure that it was Bill who called his police friends and had me rousted."

"Bill isn't the only one that values his privacy. Most everyone in that room has connections to people in the highest level of city government. No one else was ever to have learned of that group, its meeting location or the stories told there. I am not sure how you found out about us, but it wasn't hard to deduce that you didn't just stumble into that room by accident."

"So then if you knew I was an outsider, why did you continue to tell your stories with me in attendance."

"That was our wives' ideas. They wanted to find out exactly who you were and how much you knew before shutting you down."

I turned toward Marylyn, who had a big smile on her face. "And I assume that the night before last was just a scouting expedition?"

"Oh, I wouldn't say that. For my part, I enjoyed everything we did. And Fred got quite a kick out of it as well when I relayed the story to him. He was a little disappointed when I told him that you did not get to cum inside me. But he still enjoyed eating me regardless."

"Now, I am totally confused," I said as I turned back towards Fred. "From your story, I got the impression that you hated the taste of cum. Now Marylyn says that you were disappointed that you didn't get to taste mine. How do you reconcile the two statements?"

Fred kind of hung his head a little bit in shame, I guess, but then Marylyn spoke sharply to him. "Tell him, slave."

That seemed to perk Fred right up. "I wasn't lying when I said that I hated the taste of cum. I suppose some men enjoy it, but it is nasty. Now precum is another matter. That is just sweet and warm on the tongue, and I could eat that all night long. But a big glob of white stuff is completely a different taste. It tastes a little acidic, and it burns the back of your throat when it goes down. And that bitter taste stays in your mouth sometimes even after you have brushed your teeth. In short, it is about the worst taste you could imagine. If you hang around with these women though, you will get to experience it for yourself. You might want to heed my warning."

"So then, if you hate it so much, why were you disappointed that Marylyn didn't bring you home some?"

"Because she goes wild when she makes me ingest what a lover has left inside her. She goes to a whole different level of sadism. And she takes particular delight in humiliating me, which I love."

"Wow, I have to tell you that I thought the two of you were divorced. You were so convincing standing up there with that microphone in your hand and telling your sob story. You should perhaps try acting for a living."

Fred looked at me and cocked his head to the side as if he was studying me for some reason. "Take a good look at this woman beside me," he said. "Do you think even for one minute that I would be so stupid as to divorce her? And if you ever get the opportunity to fuck her without those rings, you will become so addicted that you would do anything for another, go at her pussy. Of course, she had made it plain that my tiny cock will not enter her again. But still, I can hope she might change her mind someday. In the meantime, I will take whatever she gives me, pleasure, or pain."

"In any event, it would not be good for you to return to the meetings," Marylyn announced. "The next time you show up there, it will not just be your camera that gets broken. If you are really good, perhaps one of us will invite you to a private party as long as you don't try to record or tape anything that happens there."

"So, how do I finish my article?"

"Do what all journalists do, make something up. Just don't use anything that would divulge our identities. And by the way, Marci wanted me to give you this." She handed me an envelope and then took

Fred's arm and urged him towards the door. Fred turned back and offered me his hand, which I took in a firm handshake.

"I enjoyed meeting you, and I hope that you can understand our position. Some people have to know what goes on in our lives. Otherwise, the humiliation factor would not be as good. But we can't afford for the general public to find out."

I nodded as he opened the door to leave. Marylyn turned back to me and said loud enough for Fred to hear. I enjoyed the Popsicle. Maybe we will get a chance to do it again." And like Marcie, two nights previous she blew me a kiss as she went out my door.

I was still shaking my head in disbelief as I poured my third cup of coffee. I picked up the almost empty pack of cigarettes and shook one out into my hand. As I drew the smoke into my lungs, I opened the envelope Marylyn had given to me. All that was written on the note inside was an address and 11 p.m.

The day slowly passed as I anticipated what I was going to do that evening. When the clock showed that it was nearly 10 p.m., I got in my car and set the GPS for the address on the note. I was unfamiliar with the area that it led me to and was surprised to notice that the properties along the way became larger and more expensive. When the artificial female voice told me to turn right and that I was at my destination, I pulled into a long curved drive, which was lighted on both sides. Large trees lined it, making an almost perfect canopy that I was sure even in the daylight would have blocked most of the sunlight. The house was set well back in from the road, although house was not the correct word. The mansion would have been more accurate, and I felt a little anxiety begin building in my stomach as I wondered what I might have gotten myself into. There were marked spaces to park, and I selected one marked guest and pulled into it.

Before I could exit the car, two uniformed guards arrived and demanded to see my identification. I showed them my driver's license, and I was told to get out of the car and turn around to be searched. They were thorough as they patted every area where I might have been able to conceal a weapon. When satisfied that I was harmless, one of the guards announced that they were expecting me and showed me to the door.

I did not even need to knock on the door before it was opened by a maid in formal attire right down to the lace cap on her head and the shiny black heels on her feet. Something was familiar about her, but I could not put my finger on it. She told me to follow her, and I walked behind, watching her satin-covered ass sway from side to side seductively. I was led into a very large living room, although from its size, it could as well have been a lounge in a large club of some kind. Marci came forward and excused her maid and then took my hand in greeting.

"It is so nice that you could join us tonight. Bill has been anxious to apologize to you for last evening. She then hooked her arm in mine and led to a large leather-covered sofa. I noticed a curtain had been pulled across part of the room. I sat down, and Marci sat close beside me. She handed me a cigarette and put one between her lips. Bill hates me smoking in the house. That is the main reason I do it."

"Where is Bill?" I asked.

"Oh my, I almost forgot about him." She reached over and pressed a button, and the curtain started to pull back. I could not believe my eyes, for there was Bill naked as a jaybird sitting on a tall kitchen stool. His legs were in terrible pain. I knew that because they were restrained in the same way, mine had been two nights previous. A large ball gag was in his mouth and was fastened by leather strips that went behind his head. Vicious-looking clamps were attached to his nipples, and heavyweights dangled from the clamps. I could see pain line his face, and his forehead was wrinkled in agony.

I looked over at Marci, and she gave me a big smile. "We thought this would be better than a verbal apology. She stood up and began removing her dress as she bent down and took my lips with her own. Once you have finished fucking me properly, I thought you might like to spend a little time using one of my whips on his bare body. And of course, he will be obligated to clean whatever you deposit into my cunt out with his tongue. Come now, get out of your clothes. We don't want to keep the poor man waiting all night." And she reached for the buttons on my shirt.

With a sly smile, she continued to undress me, her hands deftly unbuttoning my shirt as I kicked off my shoes and shed the rest of my clothes. She led me over to where he was kneeling, blindfolded and bound, waiting obediently.

She climbed onto the bed, pulling me with her, and guided me inside her. I lost myself in the feeling of her, the warmth and wetness of her body enveloping me, as she moved beneath me.

After a few moments, she reached for one of her whips, a slender length of leather that she wielded with expert precision. She trailed it over his chest and back, leaving a trail of goosebumps in its wake. With each strike, he flinched but did not cry out, maintaining his silence as she had commanded.

When we were both sated, she climbed off of me and gestured for him to come closer. He obeyed, crawling to the edge of the bed where she sat. Without a word, she pushed him down onto his hands and knees, pulling him close and positioning him so that he was facing my still-glistening sex.

"Clean her," she commanded, and he did not hesitate, leaning in and beginning to lick and suck at my folds, eagerly consuming every last drop of me.

As he did so, she leaned back against the pillows, watching with a satisfied smile as I tangled my fingers in his hair, pulling him closer and guiding his movements.

When we were finished, she dismissed him, and he left without a word, still blindfolded and bound. She turned to me, a wicked glint in her eye.

"Until next time," she murmured, and I knew that I would be back for more.

The End.

If you have questions, comments, or suggestions you would like to make, feel free to email me directly. wandapters1@yahoo.com

Don't miss out!

Visit the website below and you can sign up to receive emails whenever Wanda Peters publishes a new book. There's no charge and no obligation.

https://books2read.com/r/B-A-COFL-COTGB

BOOKS 2 READ

Connecting independent readers to independent writers.

Did you love *Cuckold's Anonymous*? Then you should read *Tales of Love Romance and Marriage*[1] by Wanda Peters!

[2]

This book is a series of stories about husbands, wives, and lovers who find happiness in and out of marriage. I hope you find some happiness in reading it.

---

1. https://books2read.com/u/47JrKN

2. https://books2read.com/u/47JrKN

Also by Wanda Peters

10 Reasons You Should Cuckold Your Husband
Cruel Wife, Slave Husband
Embracing My Inner Bitch
Erotic Short Stories of Dominance and Submission
My Evil Step-Sister Returns Illustrated
Cuckolded By A Stranger, An Erotic Novel
Cuckolded By His Boss
The Hot Wife Club
Cuckolded and Bound for Punishment
Cuckolded By My Best Friend
Cuckold's Anonymous
An Anniversary To Remember
My Wife's Surprise
Terrified of Bondage A Wife in Peril
Training Her Cuckold Husband
A Little Devil in Georgia
His Mother's Advice
Addicted To High Heels or A Slave To My Wife's Boots
The Huntress
A Wedding to Remember
Evil Under a Western Sky
The Number Four Reason You Should Cuckold Your Husband
Cuckolding The Bootlicker
Bondage and Discipline 101
Tales of Love Romance and Marriage

Tales of Love, Romance and Marriage
The Evil Therapist Returns
Cracks in the Vow Six Stories of Love's Demise
Two Books Of Domination And Legal Thrillers
An Old Flame For Ava
An Interview With An Erotic Writer
Bound For Desire
The Awakening- Susan's Path to Sensual Empowerment

About the Author

I have been writing erotica for the past 15 years. Most of what I write is about dominant wives and submissive husbands. Occasionally I will write a book about a submissive woman because that seems to be what some readers want.

www.ingramcontent.com/pod-product-compliance
Lightning Source LLC
Chambersburg PA
CBHW060446160726

47992CB00003B/1106